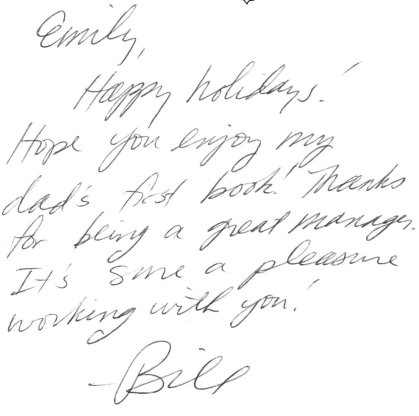

Emily,

Happy holidays.
Hope you enjoy my
dad's first book! Thanks
for being a great manager.
It's sure a pleasure
working with you.

— Bill

BILL BENNETT

THE CHRISTMAS

GIFT

BURGESS ADAMS PUBLISHING

Burgess Adams Publishing
5406 West 11000 North
Suite 103-311
Highland, UT 84003-8942
(801) 770-2610

Manufactured in the United States of America

ISBN 978-0-9825606-1-7

Dedication

This story is dedicated to
all those people
who have offered an apology,
no matter how difficult, or
have given forgiveness,
deserved or not…

…or are striving to do so

" *We cannot live only for ourselves. A thousand fibers connect us with our fellow man.* "

-Herman Melville

Prologue

"I want to get him, and I want to get him good!" the man growled. His face was red and he seemed ready to leap out of his chair.

The lawyer was expressionless as he sat across the table from the man and waited for him to finish. He thought his client seemed expectant, as though he would join in the threat like boys in grade school on their way to settle a score. The lawyer, however, said nothing, sitting with his pen and his empty pad of paper in front of him.

The man was dressed in an older suit that clearly had seen little use. He owned a construction company, and having grown up in the business, usually wore jeans and the logo T-shirt appropriate for the days he spent on the sites of his open projects. His good nature was overshadowed today by an uncharacteristic anger. He had come to the law offices on a mission. He had been wronged, and he intended to deal with it, wearing his dated suit like a coat of armor to show he meant business.

The man pursed his lips, stuck out his jaw and shook his head saying, "This guy will never mess with me again!"

More silence.

He now was mad at his attorney in addition to the person and the crime he had come to discuss.

"Well, you're the lawyer; don't you think we can get him?" the man demanded.

"Mr. Tanner," the lawyer began with a controlled calmness, "I would first like to find out what happened and why…"

"How he messed with me?!" the man interrupted.

"Yes, Mr. Tanner..." the lawyer said as he removed his glasses and ran his fingers through his graying hair. "How he 'messed' with you. Let's discuss both what he did and why he did it, and then we can decide what would be the right thing to do."

For the next hour, the lawyer listened to Mr. Tanner tell the tale of how he had been wronged. He heard a lot of the 'what,' but while he intently followed the story, he never heard a 'why.'

Mr. Tanner finally fell quiet, waited a long while, and then asked, "Well, have I got a great case?"

The lawyer stood and walked to the window, put his hand on the sill, and just gazed. His stare was aimless as he looked through the suspended Christmas wreath, identical to the ones in each window of their law firm.

"Mr. Tanner," the lawyer said wearily, "What's happened is not clear cut, and in fact is the kind of thing some people just walk away from and forget. I realize you are offended and being a man of action, you want to do something about it. But I think you should first understand why he did this to you. His intent may not be what you think. Perhaps you could settle this by talking it out?"

The lawyer turned and peered over his glasses at Mr. Tanner in a way that changed his last statement into a question.

Mr. Tanner was visibly frustrated. "Look, I want to hire you to sue this guy. Do you want the work or don't you?

The lawyer paused, and taking a breath said, "Not necessarily. I don't like to see people sue each other over a misunderstanding."

With that, he started to turn back to his aimless gaze out the window, and as he did, his eyes fell on the single picture hanging on the wall.

The sketch was very good in a simple sort of way. The scene was of a lake with a craggy shoreline, creating a serene beauty that only the randomness of nature could provide. In the distance, old mountains, characterized by their rolling contours, rose from the horizon in an impressive backdrop. They cradled a single thin but majestic waterfall which cascaded across layers of hills and then poured into the lake. In the foreground, a weathered dock stretched over the narrow, rocky beach a short distance into the water. At its end sat two boys, feet dangling over the edge, holding fishing poles, seemingly oblivious to the artist as they discussed some item of importance to their world.

The lawyer stopped and looked intently at the picture for a while. He knew this work of art intimately well, having studied each of its thoughtful pencil strokes an untold number of times. He had discovered its several subtle images and assessed its many meanings so often that if he had any artistic talent of his own, he could have flawlessly recreated the piece without looking at it. Yet today, after contemplating the picture, he found something new – or at least, something that suddenly enlightened him in his effort to assist Mr. Tanner. He smiled at the illustration and then turned and quickly walked back to the table and sat down, leaning forward, hands folded in front of him.

"Mr. Tanner, I have an idea. If you let me tell you a story… a story about that picture on the wall behind me, I'll take your case if you still want me to. Do we have a deal?"

Mr. Tanner looked up at the picture, seeing no apparent relevance to his situation, and refocused his gaze on the lawyer with a grunt. "I don't really have time for a story. I just want to talk about my case."

"Please," the lawyer said sincerely, "Hear me out. I promise it will be worth it." He stared unflinchingly into Mr. Tanner's eyes.

Without saying anything, Mr. Tanner leaned back in his chair with a sigh, looked at his watch, and folded his arms across his chest. He took a second look at his watch just to make the point. The lawyer took this as a sign – a reluctant sign, but a sign nonetheless – to tell his story.

hapter 1

Scott was new. Of course, he was not new at being new.

Scott had been the new kid many times. In fact, about every three years, Scott was the new kid. As his father was transferred from one location to another in his company, Scott's family would pack up their belongings and follow along, prepared to begin again in the next community.

This time he was new in Maple Grove.

Scott was fine with it. He and his two sisters were close, both in age and heart, and with the help of their mother, they viewed their moves as adventures.

He liked most people. He never felt the need to be popular or the center of attention. In the little society called 'school,' there were the castes that had formed as in every generation. There were the jocks who liked to hit each other in the arm in the hall. There were the nerds who for some reason all wore glasses and were friends with either the science or math teacher. There were the 'freaks' who each sported a T-shirt with their favorite band, all the shirts being black and including at least one picture of a skull. Scott called the great remaining mass, the 'normals.' They had no identity as a group, did not congregate, and were just, well, normal. Scott was a 'normal' and was content with it.

Despite all this, Scott was nervous the first week of school, as he always was. He was not so much worried about fitting in as standing out. Lots of clues called out the new kid. Yet, this time the styles seemed about the same, so his pants and shirt were acceptable. His hair looked about like every other boy's hair. Everyone talked about the same – no different accents that marked Scott as an outsider, no different slang. It seemed it would all be better than he expected.

Usually, he would find friends in the first few weeks. In the lunchroom, on the playground, or in class, he would run into someone that laughed at the same joke or seemed interested in the same topic and that person would become his first friend. It would lead to a new circle that shared common interests.

This time friendship would come quickly – the first day – and it would be in the lunchroom.

And, as usual, there were some that didn't like him.

Scott was not sure why anyone wouldn't care for him, aside from perhaps his shortcomings in throwing a long bomb, knowing the cover story of the last <u>Popular</u>

<u>Science</u>, or naming all the members of the
Grateful Dead. But with the 'normals' these
were not terribly important, and so these skills
and facts went mostly unnoticed by Scott.
Still, there were always a few he managed to
rub the wrong way.

This time, those rubs would also come
quickly, also the first day, and also in the
lunchroom. This time, the one that clearly
would not like him was Ben.

On Scott's first day in sixth grade, he was
in the lunch line behind a boy who looked
three grades older than him. At first he
thought it was a teacher, but he noticed the
long wispy hairs that were a poor attempt at
growing side-burns and realized this person
must be a student. This, he would learn, was
Ben – or, as he was known by the students,
'Big Ben,' 'Ben-ja-maniac,' 'Ben-Hurt,' and a
myriad of other names. As they pushed their
trays down the line, Scott could hear Ben
making derogatory comments and laughing
about the food choices, comparing each to a

different item on a long list of unappetizing images. When they came to the dessert section, Scott leaned as far as he could under the sneeze guard to grab a piece of Boston Cream pie. The movement caught Ben's eye, and he turned and saw Scott put the pie on his tray.

Ben pondered the pie a second, and then leaned into the dessert section to find another. Scott could see Ben's eyebrows furrow as he discovered what Scott already knew —that he had taken the last piece.

Ben never looked at Scott's face. He just reached down, took Scott's pie, put it on his own tray, and walked on, never breaking his conversation with his friends.

Scott was not one to pick a fight, or necessarily run from one either. He had come home with a bruise or two over the years, but frankly, did not find much worth fighting about. This was the case with the pie. Scott stiffened in anger, but then let it go and looked back at the dessert cooler. He picked out a piece of chocolate cake which had probably looked better the day before. Given that this was the first day of school, he wasn't sure why they had day-old cake, but it was tolerable. He briefly looked at his pie moving down the line with Ben toward the cash register, thought how much he liked Boston Cream, and then reminded himself it was no big deal. He paid and found a place to sit by himself.

He had only been seated at the end of the long folding lunch table a few seconds when a boy about his age with unruly hair and freckles sat next to him. He set down his tray with his macaroni and cheese, but wanted to talk to Scott first.

"So, you fed Ben today?"

"Huh?" Scott said, as he looked up with a mouthful of meatloaf.

"You fed Ben. You let him take your pie. Good call."

Scott swallowed, took a drink from his milk carton, and asked, "Why was it a good call?"

"Because you would have let him or you would have worn it. That's Ben Jackson. He's not human. Me and Jake checked once and we found out he was made in a lab."

Scott smiled and looked at the boy, who grinned back.

"My name is Andy. Welcome to Forestdale School. Beware of Ben, that's all I gotta say."

"Hi, Andy. My name is Scott. And... I'm not afraid of Ben."

"Yeah, Bobby Cooper said that too."

"Yeah? What happened to him?"

"No one knows. He just disappeared. We think Ben ate him."

Scott looked at Andy with a disgusted twist of his mouth. Taking a bite of his green beans, he offered, somewhat sarcastically, "Maybe he moved away?"

"Well, his parents did," said Andy, looking down and dipping into his macaroni and cheese. "But we think they moved because Ben ate him."

"You know, somehow I don't believe you."

"Yeah," Andy laughed, "I don't believe me either, but you're the new kid and we have to see how dumb you are. You didn't buy it, so you pass."

Scott and Andy talked as they finished their lunches. After dropping off their trays, they walked out to the field for recess.

Andy introduced Scott to a group of boys and soon they started a basketball game. Scott got the ball and was about to pass it when he heard a commotion and stopped. Looking over to the next court, he saw a crowd of kids gathering.

"Leave it alone, Scott," Andy cautioned, but Scott walked over to see what was going on. As he approached, he could see Ben's head sticking up above all the other children's.

He wormed his way through the growing crowd and could see Ben and a few like him surrounding a boy they were pushing back and forth.

"We had the court first," Ben said in a mocking voice, obviously imitating something the taunted boy had complained to them about.

Ben barked more firmly, "We can play anywhere we want!"

"This is what he does," Andy whispered. "He wants what you got, and he takes it. Later, he kills you. He's buried at least four kids under the baseball diamond." Scott ignored him as he watched for another minute and saw that the boy looked scared. Without a word, Scott walked into the circle.

"C'mere." Scott said to the boy. "Come play with us." Scott motioned with his head for the boy to follow him.

The crowd went quiet as Ben stared at the scene unfolding before him. Obviously, Scott had crossed into a place no one in the school had dared go before.

"Whoa, it's 'Pie-Man'," Ben said. Scott cringed as he walked away, knowing that Ben now recognized him. *This was not good*, he thought. He tried to shrink his head into his body as he walked, but he could not retract it far enough.

He felt hot breath on his neck. "Here to save your little buddy?" Ben said, loud enough for all to hear. Scott just kept walking with the boy. As they got to their court, they ignored Ben and started playing. Within seconds, however, Ben stood in front of Scott.

"We want to play on *this* court…" Ben said, pausing and pointing at the ground for effect, "…with *your* ball, Pie-Man…" gesturing toward the ball under Scott's arm, "which is now, *my* ball." Ben grabbed the ball and immediately went for a layup, body-slamming Scott to the ground as he went. He lay there as Ben and his friends started to play, then slowly got up and walked off, casting a frustrated backwards glance at his lost territory. Andy and others quickly came to his side.

"Hey, way to go! Way to stand up to him!"

"That was standing up to him? He took our court, he took your ball, he knocked me over and I didn't do anything about it."

Scott looked back at the court that Ben and his friends had already deserted and said sarcastically, "Yeah, way to go."

"Well, most kids just start crying," Andy said with authority. "Have a breakdown, right here on the playground. They need counseling later. By comparison, you're a hero."

Despite Andy's assurances of Scott's intense bravery, he felt more like a loser.

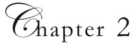

Chapter 2

And so it began. Scott built a new group of friends, with Andy as his best. But every day, there was Ben. Sometimes it was helping himself to Scott's food. Sometimes it was knocking him over in the hall. Sometimes it was pushing his books out of his arms as he walked to the bus. Scott never knew what was coming, but he imagined that each night Ben plotted the attack for the next day.

He did find that every time something happened, he was surrounded with other kids, who consoled him by telling 'Ben Stories.'

First, there were the ridiculous claims:

"He's been in the 6th grade for five years."

"One time, my friend saw him beat up eleven kids from another school all at once."

"I heard the police are afraid of him and had to call in the FBI to arrest him, but he escaped."

"His house is actually built over a cave where he and his gang go down and take kids apart and stick them back together with different arms and legs and stuff."

Then there were the more troubling assertions:

"He was a 'juvie' and spent six months in a detention center for punching a teacher in the face."

"His parents hit him when he's bad. Kids have seen his scars in the locker room."

"He's got a disease in his brain that makes him act crazy and want to kill people."

In response to each story, Scott just ignored the gossips, or looked at them with obvious skepticism. He figured none of these were entirely true. But he did know one thing, and that was that he, and every kid in the school, hated Ben.

One day, just before Halloween, he was eating the turkey lunch special. He left his spoon in the mashed potatoes while he picked up his pumpkin-shaped cookie. Before he could do anything, a hand shot out from over his shoulder and hit the end of the spoon, flipping mashed potatoes up in his face. He whirled to find Ben and his friends standing there laughing. With the white potatoes clinging to his nose and ears, Scott jumped off the bench and stood in front of Ben, fists clenched and body taut, as the entire cafeteria began chanting, "Fight! Fight! Fight!"

Then, Scott did something he had never done before, by saying something he had never said, and soon would wish he hadn't.

"Ben," he yelled with his teeth gritted. "I hate you, everybody hates you. Why don't you leave us alone?"

Something happened. It was so fast, no one but Scott saw it. He stared at Ben as he said those words and saw that for a split second, Ben's eyes changed. They were not laughing and they were not mad. They were not anything Scott had ever seen on Ben.

They were hurt.

It was more than just a quick offense. It was as though Scott got a brief glimpse into a world full of pain and fear and weariness. Yet, just as quickly as the look came, it was gone, replaced with a taunting, sarcastic smile as Ben mocked Scott:

"Oooo, he hates me. I'm so sad. I may not get a Christmas present from Pie-Man." All Ben's friends laughed as they walked away. Scott watched Ben turn and though he did not hear Ben say anything else, he could swear he saw something different in Ben's walk. Somehow, in the way he carried himself, he looked insecure.

hapter 3

Over the next few days, Scott mentally replayed Ben's brief but painful reaction, trying to decipher what he saw. It was not a look that would have seemed so unusual for anyone else in those circumstances. But for Ben, it was out of place. The more Scott pondered, the more he was filled with another emotion – regret.

Why should he feel bad? Ben had made at least one part of each day miserable for Scott.

One benefit, however, was that Scott's social status had climbed a couple notches from the lunchroom confrontation (somewhat offset by how silly he had looked with mashed potatoes hanging from his face). He kept reasoning with himself, using all the justifications offered by his friends. It worked briefly each time he thought it through. However, soon after each self-counseling session, the discomfort in his gut returned.

Halloween arrived. Scott, Andy and his friends had a long debate as to whether, at eleven, they were too old to trick-or-treat. They decided this was it – the last year – and a small portion of their time was spent on planning costumes, with the greater effort on the characteristics of treat bags that could hold the most candy, the streets that would produce the highest yield, and how soon they could begin in the evening. The decisions were made: pillow cases were the best all-round solutions for capacity and strength; the target would be medium-grade neighborhoods where the houses were still reasonably close but homeowners would likely buy the bigger candy bars; 6:00 PM would be the start time. The boys bought moppy wigs, put on their suits, made cardboard guitars, and became the Beatles – with a few extra band members.

The night began with an aggressive attack: the 'Fab-Seven' started on the far side of town where the homes were old and close together with no fences, allowing for fast transitions from door to door. They were polite at every house, but wasted no time with chit-chat.

Many homeowners frustrated that plan by exclaiming, 'Oh, the Beatles! Now, which one is Paul?" The boys would try to explain that no one was anyone in particular other than Andy, who had brought his brother's drumsticks and was feeling rather stupid for choosing to be Ringo – no one ever asked about him. As the evening wore on, he threw the drumsticks in the pillow case and every time someone asked the 'Paul' question, he would immediately respond by yelling out "I am!" He did this partly to get a little more attention, but more importantly to get the dumb question answered quickly so they could hit the next house.

As the bags filled, the between-house sprints changed to a walk, and the group would occasionally pause under street lights to pick out the best of the haul for a snack. During one such break, while the rest of the group sat on the curb and began an impromptu candy trading session, Scott casually surveyed the street in front of them. It was the peak of the evening and the many small troupes of super-heroes, hobos and hippies were almost back-to-back as they worked the neighborhoods.

What held his attention was one particular house directly across from them. The lights were on, the standard cardboard pumpkin and black cat were taped to the window, and the front door was open with only the storm door in its place. Inside were a brightly lit hall and a big bowl still brimming with candy on a table by the entrance.

However, as trick-or-treaters left the house next door, they stopped and whispered something among themselves, looking at this particular house. They sprinted past the property to the next one, screaming in terror. Others yelled something, followed by derisive laughter as they too passed. Still more saw the clusters of children before them skip the home, and shrugging their shoulders, did the same. Occasionally, he saw what looked like an older sibling, accompanying a young princess or bumblebee, stop their little brother or sister as they headed toward the house. The children looked up at their escort, who, without a word, tugged them along the sidewalk in front of the house, moving on to the next target. Once, he heard one of these older brothers say out loud in frustration, "Because! That's why. Ask me about it when we get home."

"Hey Andy," Scott called. "C'mere a minute."

"Yes, Guv'ner?" Andy said as he walked over to Scott, using his weak rendition of a cockney British accent.

Scott rolled his eyes. "Andy, that's Mary Poppins, not the Beatles."

"What's up?" Andy asked normally, feeling stupid once again.

"What's with that house? You can see people are home. I can even see the candy from here. How come nobody's going up to their door?"

Andy dropped his voice to a whisper. "That place... is where Ben lives. Nobody wants a one-way trip up there. Heck, the candy they're giving out is probably stuff he stole from other kids."

Scott kept looking at the house, amazed that every single group passed it by. "I'm sure Ben isn't even there. It must be his mother handing it out – or not handing it out. Why don't we just go up? They have so much candy she would probably give us each three pieces."

"You can't do that!" Andy scolded Scott. "It's not just the danger – it's the… look of it. You can't trick-or-treat Ben's house. He's off-limits. When we were little and our parents drove by his here, we would hold our breath until we passed his property. Nobody ever goes there."

"Why did you hold your breath?"

"I dunno. Seemed like the thing to do."

"Don't you think his mother feels bad?" Scott asked. "All that candy and nobody comes to their door?"

"Don't know and don't care," Andy said. "I just know I am not going up there!"

"Come on," Scott said. "Just once. We're a big group. Nobody's going to hurt us." Scott smiled at Andy. "You scared, scaredy-cat?"

Andy replied immediately. "Yes!"

Scott gave it up. The boys moved on, following suit with the rest of the groups walking by Ben's house.

Scott looked in as they passed. He wondered what Ben did on a night like this. Did he go out with friends? Did he hide in the bushes and steal kids' candy? Was he still thinking about what Scott said to him, the way Scott was?

Chapter 4

Scott gorged himself with his Halloween haul as did everyone else. He did not eat a thing all the next day, and for a few short hours, he committed himself to a life of vegetarianism. By Sunday, his stomach was settling and he looked forward to their traditional family dinner.

However, nothing seemed interesting. Scott picked lightly at his food, lost in his thoughts about Ben. He was curious and bothered. When he'd told Ben everyone hated him, he hadn't really known that – he'd just said it in anger to hurt him. However, it was looking like everyone really did. Not even candy would draw kids to his home.

"Scott," his dad said after dinner, "come into the kitchen, please, and help me with the dishes while Mom and your sisters take a nap."

His father handed him a dish towel and said, "I'll wash, you dry."

After a few minutes of simple talk about Halloween, his father asked him, "What's on your mind, Scott? You seem far away today."

"Nothing," Scott said.

After a minute of silence, his father asked, "You excited for Thanksgiving and Christmas?"

"Kind of."

His father said no more, which was as good as asking again.

"Okay," Scott said, realizing that his father was going to be persistent. "I feel bad about something I said. There's this kid, Ben, who tries to make me miserable every day."

Scott then told him the stories of all the encounters he had with Ben. "So, when this thing with the mashed potatoes happened, I told him that me and all the kids hated him."

His father stopped washing, wiped his hands, and then turned and leaned back against the counter, facing Scott.

After a few moments of contemplation, he asked, "So, think about it. Do you?"

"What?"

"Hate him. Do you really hate Ben?"

"Yeah... No, not really. But I hate what he does! I hate worrying about it every day."

His father laughed. "That, I get." He then became more serious. "But words can be a pretty powerful weapon."

"I know," Scott said. "I felt like I had a weapon. Dad, when I said it, I saw something that happened so quickly, I don't think anyone else even noticed. It was in his eyes. It was like I hit Ben, even though I didn't."

"Well," his father said, "you obviously hurt Ben, but he's trying to hide it."

"Well, he's hurting me every day."

"Physically?"

"No," Scott consented, "not really. He's just bothering and embarrassing me."

"Yes, and that's not good either. Ben is out of line." His father paused for a moment, and then added, "What do you want to do about it?"

"Oh, I'm fine. I'm not the only kid he bothers, and my friends always try to make me feel better." He paused. "Yesterday, someone told me Ben was a runaway from an island of half-men, half-gorillas."

Scott let out a small laugh, expecting his dad to at least offer a smile. However, he was chagrinned when he saw the serious, sad look on his father's face. He immediately felt as he did when he told Ben he hated him.

"I'll be alright," Scott said quietly.

"I know you will, Scott," his father said. "And that's important. But that is not what I meant when I asked you the question."

Scott looked up, confused.

His father continued, "What I meant was: what are you going to do about how bad you feel for hurting Ben?"

They sat quietly together, Scott knowing where this was going, and his father knowing he knew it.

"Scott," his father said thoughtfully, "I don't know what makes Ben do what he does, but I do know that when people say ridiculous things like that about someone, people become kind of a mob. They don't really think. They jump on some crazy comment and group up against the person about whom it was said."

Scott told his father about watching Ben's house on Halloween. He winced as he told him, just as his father did as he heard it.

His father looked at the floor and shook his head.

"That's exactly what I mean, Scott. A few people start a rumor and look what it does. Can you imagine what his family feels like... what Ben feels like? When a person thinks everyone is against them, sometimes they do things to protect themselves and hide their feelings."

"Don't you think Ben deserved it?"

"No, I don't. I think Ben needs to be dealt with, but not that way." He paused, and then said, "Let me ask you something. Why does Ben act like that?"

"I don't know. I have no idea. Nobody does."

"Well, why don't you find out?"

"How?"

"Well, do you still feel bad about saying you hated him?"

"Yup," Scott said with a sigh, "I feel even worse now that we're talking about it."

His father reached out and tousled Scott's hair. "It won't go away until you make it right. Do you know how to do that?"

"Yeah," Scott said without enthusiasm, knowing what he needed to do and dreading it. "I need to say I'm sorry."

"That's right. When you do, why don't you ask Ben why he does what he does? Find a time when he's not around his friends, so he doesn't feel any need to perform in front of them."

"Yeah. Okay." Then, after a pause, he asked, "Dad, can I take karate first?"

"Scott…"

"I know, I know."

I'm a dead man, Scott thought.

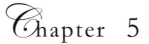

Chapter 5

"You're going to what!?" Andy exclaimed in disbelief the next day. "Hey, maybe if he tears your tonsils out first, you won't have to say it!" The two boys walked to school with Scott discussing how he would apologize, and Andy responding with example after example of what Ben would do in return.

"What are you apologizing for anyway?" Andy asked, taking a new tack. Then, he mocked what Scott might say: "'I'm sorry I didn't have more mashed potatoes so you could hit other kids too?' 'I'm sorry you had to reach over so far to hit the spoon?' 'I'm sorry I had the nerve to get mad when you trashed me in front of everybody?'"

Andy got serious. "What's the deal? What was so wrong with what you did? He deserved that, except times a hundred."

"I just don't feel right," Scott said. "Even though he was a jerk, I still shouldn't have said me and everybody hated him."

"Well, I think the score is not even close to even, and you and every kid in the school are on the losing end. I don't get it."

However, that school day didn't go the way it had for the last few months. Ben walked by Scott in the hall and did not look at him. In the lunch room, Ben was the same old Ben to everyone, except that he didn't come near Scott.

He thought for the next few days that perhaps he would not have to face up to the apology. But his stomach still hurt and he wasn't happy. For some reason he didn't understand, Ben didn't want to see Scott. And, for a reason he understood clearly, Scott didn't want to see Ben. It wasn't that he was scared of him. He felt safer from Ben than ever. It was just that when he looked at Ben, his gut reminded him of the difficult thing he had to do that was still undone. He knew he had to get it over with.

Scott decided he would go to Ben's house so it would be easier for Ben to talk, as his Dad had suggested. However, since Andy had led them around on Halloween, he couldn't remember where Ben's house was. He went to the office after school to get the address. Mrs. Martinelli, manning her post at the front desk, looked up over her reading glasses. "Hey, Scott, how are you getting along?"

"Fine, I guess," Scott said without enthusiasm. "Mrs. M, can I get an address from you?"

"Sure, Scott, whose do you need?" she asked as she grabbed the school directory.

"Ben Jackson's."

Mrs. Martinelli stopped. "Is this about the lunchroom incident?"

'*Lunchroom incident,*' Scott thought. *This thing has a name already.* He pictured the school staff sitting around with a case file on him, Ben, and the 'incident.'

"Well, yeah, sort of," Scott said, trying to avoid Mrs. Martinelli asking why he wanted it.

"Scott," she said, putting the directory back down, "Why do you want it?"

Well, that didn't take long, he thought.

"I need to do something," Scott said quietly, feeling her bearing in on his reason like a heat-seeking missile.

"Scott, I think you should let your parents handle anything about this. If you have your father or mother call, I'll give them the Jackson's phone number."

"My parents can't... shouldn't... handle this. I have to." Scott said with frustration.

Mrs. Martinelli said nothing but virtually demanded with her practiced stare that he supply more information.

Scott looked back without a word. It became a contest.

Scott lost.

"It's like this," he said uncomfortably, "I... I said something to Ben. It wasn't good. I have to apologize to him."

Mrs. Martinelli looked shocked. She sat back, eyebrows arched and pursed her lips. Slowly a smile came across her face as her look changed to approval and she reached for the directory again.

"I think it will be okay," she said, smiling. She took out a slip of paper and wrote down the address. Handing it to him she added, "He only lives a couple blocks from here."

Scott turned to leave, but stopped as Mrs. Martinelli addressed him.

"Scott," she said, but didn't say anything else. She just smiled and slightly nodded her head.

The next day was Thursday, two weeks before Thanksgiving. He had contemplated somehow delaying this visit until December, but he knew he couldn't stand it that long. After school, he began his slow trudge toward Ben's house.

While Halloween had been warm, the recent weather had suddenly turned chilly. The leaves were almost all gone from the trees and had dropped so fast, no one had raked them up yet. He scuffed through the piles of reds and yellows and browns blown across the sidewalks, paying no attention to the crackling foliage thrown by his every step. Though he loved fall, the beautiful crisp afternoon was lost on him.

He walked slowly, not wanting to beat Ben home, and not wanting to go there in the first place. His stomach churned inside him. He thought that if he threw up on the way there, he would be justified in turning and running home.

But, he knew what would happen. It would just start all over again the next day. As he replayed the mashed potato day and his angry shot at Ben, he cringed, wishing he could somehow take it back. Whatever happened, at least both the regret and anxiety that were building in him would be gone if he just followed through. He might have a broken arm, but he could convalesce in peace.

What should have been a five minute walk turned into a twenty minute shuffle.

He eventually came to the house and recognized it from Halloween evening. As he had watched the trick-or-treaters run past the home that night, he had allowed it to take on an ominous feel in his memory. But, on this pleasant fall afternoon, it looked entirely different than he remembered. It was older, but well kept and had recently been painted, the slate blue color standing out against the fall leaves. Across the entire width of the front ran a covered porch with a hanging double-seated swing suspended at one end. In each window, lace curtains had been pulled back to let the afternoon sun stream in. The steps up to the porch and the railings around it gleamed with thick coats of carefully applied white paint. Corn stalks had been leaned against the wall by the front door, surrounded by a few pumpkins at their base.

Though Scott noticed the attractiveness of the house, it fled from his mind as he approached. He felt as though he had ankle weights on each leg while he took the steps to the porch. As he came to the door, he suddenly panicked, realizing he had no plan of how to let them know he was here.

Should he knock? If he did, he would have to open the storm door first. They might hear it open and then open the front door just as he knocked, startling them. If he knocked on the storm door, the aluminum might rattle and make it sound like he was trying to break in. If he rang the bell, it might not work, but he might not know it didn't work, and then he might stand there for a long time, and they might open the door just coming out to get their paper, or going somewhere, and they would wonder 'why is this kid just standing on our porch?' He had mapped every potential second of the coming conversation, with every contingency he could imagine. How could he have missed this one, vital detail?

Finally, in a fit of confusion and fear, he used a bit of each approach, knocking on the door, ringing the bell and straining to hear if it sounded inside.

After a moment, the inside door opened, revealing a friendly-looking woman who then opened the storm door. "Yes?" she asked.

"Hi," Scott said nervously. "I'm, uh… my name is Scott. Is Ben home?"

The woman seemed a bit surprised, but smiled and opened the door wider. "Yes. Yes he is. Please come in."

She held the door for Scott and walked with him to the entrance of a bedroom in the back of the house by the kitchen.

"Ben," she called as she knocked and opened the door. "Someone is here for you." Scott looked in to see Ben lying on his bed with headphones on. He sat up, saw Scott, and gave a confused but unfriendly look. His mother left.

He ripped the headphones from his head, slapped off the stereo, and blurted out, "What do you want?"

"To talk to you."

"Why? You gonna tell on me?"

"No."

"Well, Pie Man, then what do you want?"

Scott took a breath.

"I'm sorry."

The room was silent.

"What?" Ben said after a minute.

Scott felt incredibly awkward, saying nothing for a few more moments. He thought to himself, *this is it – get it done*. With that, everything came tumbling out.

"I'm sorry. I'm sorry I said I hated you, and that others hate you. I don't really hate you and I don't think they do either. They're just all scared of you and hate what you do to them."

He stopped and breathed in relief. Whatever was coming, was worth it.

Ben looked at Scott without a word. While his face was completely expressionless, Scott could tell Ben was thinking. He sensed that Ben did not have many conversations like this.

After an incredibly long silence, Ben laid back on his bed grunting something that sounded like 'okay,' and put his headphones back on. Scott immediately realized the conversation was over and he was not going to get to ask Ben why he did the things he did. That was fine with him at first, but he realized he had not done all he committed to do, which meant the feelings would not entirely go away.

Then, he noticed something: Ben had not turned the music back on. He was laying there pretending he was listening. *He's still interested,* Scott thought. *If I can just think of something to say.*

"Well, I gotta go," Scott said slowly but loud enough to give Ben the impression he was trying to yell over his music. He knew Ben could hear him, but he didn't move. *Gotta think of something,* he thought.

Not knowing what to do, he turned and scanned the room for an idea. His eye caught a glimpse of a picture hanging on the wall by the door. It was of a duck landing on a lake with wings outstretched. It was not a print, and Scott was momentarily shocked to think Ben might have drawn this. He was about to say how good it was, when he looked around and noticed the room was full of pictures showing various things from nature to sports to airplanes. Some were done with colored pencils, some with paint, some were just sketches.

Though Scott's purpose in finding something to talk about had been to re-engage Ben, he now asked with complete surprise and sincerity: "You do these?"

Ben took the headphones off again. "What?"

Scott smiled inside knowing he had him. "You draw all these pictures?" Scott asked.

"So what?" Ben said defensively.

"Does that mean 'yes?'"

"Yeah, it does. So what?"

"They're good."

Ben just sat there. He didn't offer a reply, so Scott assumed that was the end of it. Resigning himself to the failure of the second half of his mission, he stepped out of his bedroom to leave, but as he did he heard Ben call out to him.

"Want to see more?" Ben asked with an eager tone in his voice.

hapter 6

Scott followed Ben to the basement. He looked around as they came down the stairs, noticing there were no racks or other devices where Ben and his friends pulled kids apart and put them back together with different pieces. In fact, it looked like everyone's basement. Ben went to a huge dresser and pulled out one of the wide drawers. He lifted out a sheaf of pictures.

Ben spoke in a way Scott had never heard from him. With enthusiasm he fanned through a picture collection of birds, showing him each one, but moving so fast that Scott could only briefly look at them. Then, he moved on to his bear collection, combing through ten in less than a minute.

He put them on top of a table next to the dresser, opened another drawer and said, "And this is my kid collection," spreading out a dozen pictures of children on the growing pile of sketches. They were portrayed in all kinds of different scenes.

Scott silently scanned the array of drawings. "How do you do this?" he asked.

"I don't really know." Ben said. "I'm not very good at reading or writing or math, but I've always been able to draw. When everybody in kindergarten was drawing stick figures, I was drawing people that looked like people. When I look at something I want to draw, I guess I see it like everybody else does. But then, I see it again, or deeper or something. It's kind of like I see a story. So I draw the picture, but I try to draw the story too."

Scott saw what he meant. Every picture was excellent in a technical way – shadowing, perspective, texture – all things Scott did not comprehend other than that he knew this art was unlike anything else kids their age drew. But there was even more to them than that. In each one, there was an emotion.

In one drawing, a bear was about to eat a fish it had swiped from a waterfall, but it had paused, looking over its shoulder. In the eyes, Scott could see caution, as though the bear suspected another was coming to steal his catch. In a different one, a mother deer stood eating grass with her fawn. She stood close to her young, their sides touching as they grazed. The fawn's eyes were partially closed, ignorant of anything around it other than the blissful taste of the spring grass. The mother's head was down eating as well, but her eyes were turned up to the fawn, looking at her offspring both in love and protection.

The pictures of people were even better. In one, a child was at the top of a swing's arc.

His eyes were closed, his hair blown back, and his smile one of complete joy. Recognizing the features, Scott guessed this was young Ben. He looked up at Ben, who gave him a wry smile to acknowledge his unspoken guess.

"When do you get the time to do this? Don't you play football, or wrestle alligators, or something?"

Ben darted an angry look at Scott, then stopped and laughed. "No alligators," he said.

"Well," Scott pushed, "what about sports?"

"I don't do sports. I can't."

"Why not? Your mom won't let you? You're big enough to play on the junior high team."

"I just can't," he offered with no further explanation.

He changed the subject, asking Scott, "Do you like to fish?"

"I don't know. I never fished before."

"What! Where did you grow up? It's practically against the law *not* to fish around here."

For the next hour, Ben told Scott stories of fishing. Scott was not so much interested in the stories as he was in Ben being so interested. He was not only enthusiastic, but he painted a picture with the words he used so that the scene was created in Scott's mind. He could almost see the splash of the fish as it was reeled in.

"You boys want some pie?" Ben's mother called down the stairs. Ben looked at Scott, "You want some? Promise I won't take yours, Pie-Man." Ben grinned and Scott smiled back.

"Sure, I've been wanting pie for a long time now."

Mrs. Jackson sat at the kitchen table smiling. Her eyes darted back and forth between the boys as they talked non-stop while eating their slices of pie.

After cleaning up, Scott walked to the front door to leave. As he did, Ben stood in the hall with a discomfort that seemed to indicate he wanted to say something. But, he just stared at Scott, choosing not to say whatever was on his mind.

It was okay. Scott knew what Ben wanted to say. He wanted to tell Scott he was sorry as well, but it seemed to be too hard for him.

Scott didn't need him to. He could tell Ben was sorry, and that was enough for both of them. As he left, he realized the pit that had been in his stomach for the last week was gone.

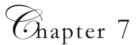hapter 7

Over the next couple weeks, Scott wandered over to Ben's house after school every few days. Sometimes they played a card game. A couple times, Ben tried to show Scott how to draw. The whole time, they talked.

At the end of the second week, Scott came by even though he had not seen Ben in school. Mrs. Jackson came to the door and looked disappointed. "Oh, Scott, I'm sorry Ben isn't here. His dad had to take him somewhere."

"Okay," he said and turned to leave, but Ben's mother called after him. "Scott, could I talk to you a minute?"

He turned and saw gentle pleading in her face "Sure," he said, and came back up the porch steps. They went into the kitchen and she got out a piece of pie, as she always did when Scott came. Scott sat in what had become his regular seat at the kitchen table.

She cut a slice and, putting it in front of Scott, joined him and took a breath.

"Scott, may I ask you something?"

"Sure," he said through a mouth full of apple pie.

"How did you and Ben come to be friends? I know he's not very nice at school."

Scott hesitated and stopped eating, not wanting to be a tattle-tale.

"It's alright," she said. "I know Ben probably pushed you around. I've been called into the school many times. That part I can guess. What I want to know is why you came here."

He told her about the mashed potato day and turned red as he repeated what he'd said. Her eyes were full of pain as he said it, sort of like Ben had looked, but she kept smiling at Scott.

"So," Scott finished, "I wanted to come say I was sorry and ask him why he did this stuff to me."

"Did you?"

"Yeah, I said I was sorry the first day I was here."

"Yes, I know about that," she said smiling. "Ben told me all about it that night when I talked to him at bedtime. He probably didn't tell you but that meant a lot to him. But, my question was: did you ask him why he's like this?"

"Nah, I never did. After we became friends, it didn't seem to matter anymore."

That seemed to please Ben's mom. She looked down into her lap a moment, and then picked up her head and asked, "May I tell you why he does those things?"

"Sure."

"Scott, Ben is sick. Sick with something that won't get better. It's a problem with his heart. It keeps him from playing sports or doing anything active. If you ever watch him play on the school field, you'll see he only does so for a minute because he gets tired. Then, he'll walk off somewhere to sit down."

Scott remembered that first day when Ben had stolen Andy's basketball. He had taken a few shots and then left the court. He thought it was because Ben didn't really want to play basketball; he had just wanted to torment Scott.

"That's how he came to spend so much time fishing in the summer, and drawing in the winter. He loves sports, but not being able to play, when he is so big and knows he could make any team he tried for, makes him mad. It worries me because he takes out his anger on others. Ben has been through many painful surgeries. Each one has taken months of recuperation and none seem to have done any good. He has endured them bravely, but when he doesn't get any better, he just gets madder."

She continued, "He doesn't really dislike anyone; he just feels a need to express his anger that way. It isn't right, but try to understand that he doesn't mean it the way it seems. Either everyone is scared of him, or they want to gang up with him as bullies. But, when the bullies come over here, they see his drawings, and somehow, he's not so interesting to them anymore. He really doesn't have any friends at all."

Scott looked at her wide-eyed, pie forgotten.

"Scott, I don't want to say what I am about to say because I know it will hurt you, but it will also help you understand. Ben tells me often that everyone hates him. He knows it inside. I think when you said those words to him, it just confirmed it."

Scott felt a pain run through him.

"Scott, I understand. Those are terrible things he does. I try to explain to him how it affects people, but somehow, between his anger and thinking everyone hates him, he can't seem to stop himself. So, everyone is scared of him, makes up stories about him, and the whole thing becomes a vicious cycle."

Then Ben's mother put her hand on his hand.

"But Scott, you're different. Somehow, you looked into Ben rather than at him. You came here and talked to him in a way that showed you liked him, and for these last few weeks, he has been different too. He's been really happy for the first time in many years. Each night, he tells me everything you two have done and talked about." She laughed as she said, "He doesn't want to leave out any details, so he takes almost as much time to tell me as you two spend together."

Scott sat quietly contemplating all he'd heard. Most likely someone had seen Ben's scars from his surgeries, and had made up the lie that his parents hit him. Somewhere along the way, his school absences from his heart condition had been fashioned into a story that he had a sickness that made him crazy. Scott decided to ask Ben's mother about one of the other rumors.

He nervously started, "Mrs. Jackson, when Ben was really mad, did he ever... hit... uh..." Scott could not bring himself to say the word.

"A teacher?" she asked softly.

Scott nodded his head.

Mrs. Jackson hesitated answering, then did so, choosing her words carefully.

"He did, Scott, but it's probably not what you think. I've tried to educate his teachers about his physical problems and most of them have been wonderfully accommodating. However, there was a gym teacher that did not..."

She paused, obviously having a difficult time saying this part. "...did not try..."

She corrected herself: "... did not seem to understand Ben's challenges. While playing basketball in class, Ben kept stopping to rest and each time he did, the gym teacher yelled louder at him, calling him 'lazy' and 'wimpy.' Ben was upset, but was controlling himself by ignoring him until the teacher ran up and yelled, 'Come on you big slug, get up and do something.'" She spoke carefully, obviously remembering every word perfectly.

"Well," she continued," Ben had just had one of his surgeries not too long before that. When they work on his heart, they have to break his rib cage. It's very painful, and his whole upper body is quite tender for several months afterwards. The teacher, I am sure not realizing what he was doing, slapped him hard on the back as he yelled at him to stand up and join the game. The pain was overwhelming to Ben, and to protect himself from another hit, he turned to push the teacher away. The teacher deflected Ben's hand and it slipped into the teacher's face, cutting his cheek."

She took a breath. "The teacher complained that Ben had attacked him. Though many children saw it happen, nobody liked Ben and so nobody spoke up. Ben had to go to juvenile court. Thankfully, there was a judge who made the effort to listen and when it was understood that Ben had undergone open heart surgery, he was cleared of any accusations. For some reason, the gym teacher never said a word of apology to him."

She paused, and then added, "But I have to tell you this about it, Scott. Ben sat in that courtroom and listened to the awful lies the teacher told about him. He never said a thing, and never lost his temper. I was very proud of him, though I know it hurt him tremendously."

She looked at Scott. "I am sure they make up all kinds of stories about that. If you ever hear one again, maybe you can straighten them out."

She smiled, and Scott smiled back, giving a nod of his head.

"Scott, Ben was not at school today because his heart had a problem. He's with his father at the hospital."

"Will he be alright?" Scott asked.

She said nothing for a minute.

Then she said, "I don't know. But, I'll tell him you came by. It will make him very happy."

Chapter 8

The next day, Ben was in school, but he looked pale and tired.

He and Scott did not usually mix much at school, but every few days, Ben would catch him in a private moment in the hall and quietly ask, "want to come by today? It's a pie day."

At first Scott thought Ben was embarrassed to be seen talking to him, but he had come to realize it was Ben that worried Scott would be embarrassed to be seen talking to *him*.

This day though, Scott did not see Ben anytime after first period.

After school, Scott jogged over to Ben's house and rang the bell. Ben answered the door. Looking worn out, he smiled and said, "I cut school again today. Come on in."

"You did not," his mother chided him. When she saw Scott, she said, "He was just tired. He needed to come home and rest." Ben quickly changed the subject. "Want to go fishing?"

"Huh? It's 24 degrees outside."

"I know. In my basement."

"You have fish in your basement?"

"Sort of. C'mere."

Ben walked slowly to the basement, his enthusiasm straining against the lack of energy he obviously felt. Scott followed, not wanting Ben to see that he had his hand out to help Ben if he fell.

When they got downstairs, Scott saw all the boxes that were usually spread across the basement had been stacked against the walls.

In the big open space, two chairs were arranged at one end. Lying on each was a fishing pole.

"My dad cleared the stuff away last night so I could teach you how to cast. We'll have to side cast because the ceiling is too low, but it will work."

Ben showed Scott the rubber casting weights on the end of each line. That day, and the next several, the two boys imagined they were on *the* lake, Ben's favorite fishing spot in the mountains, each describing the imaginary fish they caught. As they reeled in after each cast, they gave details of the fight they were having against the great trout or striped bass.

Ben's mother found numerous reasons to come down to the basement while they were there, bringing items to be set on a shelf or 'checking on something'. When she came, she would linger as long as she could to listen to the two boys.

Each day, Ben was intent on teaching him to cast, even insisting they eat their pie while they 'fished.'

One day, as they worked their lines, Ben kept urgently checking in with Scott: "Do you get it, do you feel like you can fish now?"

"I think so, but why do you care so much?"

"Promise me you'll go fishing next summer. When you do, I want you to know how."

"Sure! We gonna go to *the* lake?" as Scott had learned to reverently refer to it.

Ben paused. "Just promise me you'll go."

"Sure, I promise." Scott showed confusion, not wanting to admit to himself what Ben might be saying.

Chapter 9

Over the next few weeks, the fishing lessons became less frequent as Ben missed more days.

One week before Christmas, Scott got an idea. He went to a fishing shop and asked what was the best thing was he could buy for $10. They sold him a lure. He wanted to give Ben the gift, but he wanted to give it to him in school, in front of others. He did not care what they thought of him – he wanted Ben to know he was proud of their friendship.

He wrapped the present in appropriate boy wrapping style – no effort wasted on bows or ribbons. The wrapping paper was a page from a hunting catalog that Scott had found in their junk mail, taped with too much tape. He stuck the gift on top of his pile of books and carried it around with him from class to class, waiting to see Ben. However, Ben was not in school.

That afternoon, Scott walked the now familiar path to Ben's house. As he came down the street, he saw several cars in the parked in the driveway and more on the street in front. He walked cautiously up the steps, feeling worried but telling himself they might be having a family Christmas party. When he knocked, a strange man came to the door and simply stared at him.

"Is Ben here?" Scott asked.

The man turned and said, "Karen, it's someone for Ben." After a moment, Mrs. Jackson came to the door. Her eyes were red and swollen and she did not greet Scott with her usually ever-present smile.

As he looked at her, he felt his lip begin to quiver.

"Scott, come in a moment, would you please?"

He walked tentatively through the door. There were several clusters of people speaking in hushed tones throughout the house, frequently patting each other's backs. Their principal was there, standing with his arm around the shoulders of Mr. Jackson, who looked emptily off into nowhere.

Mrs. Jackson said, "Sit with me a minute here in the living room, would you?"

They sat on the couch and she took a big breath.

"Scott, do you remember what I told you about Ben's heart?"

Scott nodded as tears came to his eyes.

Pausing again, she said, "Well, last night, Ben's heart finally had too much. He passed away in the middle of the night in his sleep."

Scott wanted to burst out crying, but tried to hold it back. He managed to speak as he choked, "I brought Ben a Christmas present. I, uh, I…" He held out the gift, helplessly.

Mrs. Jackson took the gift from him. "Thank you Scott, that was very kind."

His voice faltered. "But, I didn't get it to him in time. I wanted to give it to him in school so everyone would see…" He could not finish his sentence.

"Scott, you meant a lot to Ben. Thank you for what you did for him. Your friendship was the greatest gift you could have ever given him."

He nodded silently, then stepped out the door and ran home. He sprinted up the stairs and sat on his bed, staring the floor. When his father came home that evening, Scott threw himself into his father's arms and sobbed late into the night.

hapter 10

That Saturday, Scott and his parents attended Ben's funeral. It was the 21st of December, but Ben's death had put all Scott's Christmas feelings on hold.

Along with all the flowers, the most prominent decorations were Ben's pictures. Through the hallways, in the foyer, and around the family meeting room, his pictures stood sentinel on their easels. If anyone doubted the depth of Ben's insights on the world, they would see him differently here. It was as though his heart was interpreted in each one. The picture Ben had showed Scott of himself as a child on a swing was positioned squarely on the table by the guest register.

Scott walked in and said hello to Ben's parents. When he shook hands with Mrs. Jackson, he started to cry. She did not release her grip and pulled him close to hug him. After she did, she whispered, "Come with me, Scott. There is something I need to show you."

They walked into the hallway. By the door to the chapel, a long display table had been set up. Arranged on the soft tablecloth were various mementos of Ben's life. His pencils, brushes, and paints were positioned as though Ben had left them there in the middle of a project just moments ago. His fishing license was on top of his tackle box. There were other tokens of his life that Scott had not had a chance to identify with Ben: a wooden train, a model car, a telescope, and more.

Mrs. Jackson put her hands on Scott's shoulders and turned him to face the center of the table. There, a box had been placed under the cloth to provide a display position of prominence above all the others. Perched on the top of this plateau was the gift Scott had brought for Ben. The top was off, leaning against the box, with the hunting magazine wrapping paper crumpled around it. Lying inside, new and pristine, was the lure that was to have been Ben's gift. In front of the display was a hand lettered sign which read, "Ben's Christmas present from Scott, his best friend of his whole life."

Scott listened to the eulogies delivered about Ben. There were parts that were familiar to him, having come to learn something about Ben in these past weeks.

There were other stories that were new. They spoke of his hopes and dreams, his challenges and frustrations. They talked about what made him sad, and what made him laugh. They talked about his love of animals and fishing and art and sports and the dog he grew up with. He realized that if Ben had died a few months earlier, and Scott had come to the funeral, he would not have had the faintest idea who they were talking about.

The talks faded into the background of Scott's mind as he contemplated his and Ben's friendship. For a while, he had been awestruck at how quickly Ben had changed as they spent time together. However, this day he realized it was not Ben that changed – it was him. He had looked deeper. It was like Ben's art. If you glanced at it quickly, you saw one thing. But, after taking time to study it, more images, more meaning came slowly into view.

The next Wednesday was Christmas, and on that morning, Scott's family arose as usual and began a great day. They sat in the den by the fire opening their stockings. They ran with excitement into the living room and gasped at the presents around the tree. They laughed around the kitchen table as they enjoyed the special Christmas breakfast Scott's mother made every year.

Scott enjoyed it all, but in moments of solitude, he felt sadness and loneliness creep back in.

That afternoon, during their family dinner, he was surprised to hear a knock on the door.

Scott's father answered and spoke to whoever was there for a moment before calling him.

"Scott, Mr. and Mrs. Jackson are here to see you."

Scott walked out, a little embarrassed at still being in his pajamas. They all stood awkwardly in the front hall. Scott's mother finally broke the silence and invited them into the living room. There were still bits of wrapping paper on the floor, and parts of a few gifts spread out in mid-assembly. The Jacksons sat on the couch next to the tree. They sat close together, leaning into each other, huddling against their still obvious grief. Scott wondered if this was hard for them to see his home, full of Christmas Day fun. On their laps, Mr. Jackson held a large, flat, wrapped present and Mrs. Jackson balanced a white cardboard box.

"We are sorry to bother you on Christmas…" Mr. Jackson said haltingly, working hard to keep his composure, "…but we wanted to carry out Ben's last wish." He was barely able to get the last words out.

Mrs. Jackson, who seemed to be more in control of her emotions, continued for her husband.

"Ben gave us a note the night after you visited for the last time. He knew how sick he was and I think he knew he only had days left. He had worked on your present so diligently for weeks and he asked me to open the note if something happened to him before Christmas. I didn't get to it until after his funeral. When I did, I read that he asked us to do two things."

Ben's father handed Scott the big package as he struggled to speak. He managed to say,

"He wanted us to give you this…" but could say no more.   Scott looked at them both as they motioned for him to open the box.

Inside was a framed drawing of a mountain lake.   The shore curled in no particular pattern, a thin beach leading into brush and trees.   In the distance, a regal waterfall cascaded through the mountains and fed the lake.   When Scott looked carefully, which he would do many times in later years, he would see camouflaged in the trees various animals grazing, hunting or laying with their young.

But what captured Scott's attention this day was a dock jutting into the lake.   At the far end of the dock were two boys sitting and fishing.   One was large, the other slight.   The boys' backs were toward the artist as they each dangled their feet in the water.   Next to each of them was something on the dock, which Scott knew was a piece of pie.   This was Ben's favorite lake, the one he had described to Scott in such vivid detail.   In one way, this was the picture of the fishing trip they never got to take. But in another, it was a picture of the trip they took every day in Ben's basement.

Mrs. Jackson continued, "He said it was just as important I give you this. I have arranged it the way he described. He also left a note for you and it's in the box." She handed him the other gift with great care, almost as though she had a last chance to touch her son.

Scott lifted the lid and looked down. Inside was a slice of Boston Cream pie on a paper plate with a plastic fork next to it. There was a paper napkin in the box as well. On the napkin, in Ben's handwriting, were the words:

"I'm sorry. And Merry Christmas. Your good friend, Ben."

hapter 11

The lawyer stopped and looked up at Mr. Tanner, whose eyes were as red as his. After a minute of quiet, Mr. Tanner softly asked, "Well, did you go fishing?"

"We did," the lawyer said, realizing with a smile that Mr. Tanner had already figured out that he was Scott. "I went fishing that next summer with my dad. As we were leaving that morning, my father asked me if it would be okay if we invited Ben's father to come too. We did, and he came, and we went to *that* lake and sat on *that* dock and talked of

Ben all day," Scott said, gesturing toward the painting.

"We went back the next summer, and the next, and every summer until Ben's dad passed away twenty five years later. During that time, I grew up, got married, and had boys of my own who started joining us. Eventually, we bought the land upon which that dock sits and built a cabin. Still to this day, more than forty years later, every summer my boys bring their families to the cabin and my father, my children, my grandchildren and I spend a day together fishing. We call it 'Ben's Day.'"

Scott Stewart looked lost in his memories for a second, and then added, "Mr. Tanner, I told you this because… "

"Stop, please," Mr. Tanner said kindly. "Let me give this man a call and talk to him. I'll try to understand why he did what he did before I do anything else."

He stood, put on his coat and began to leave.

Then, he paused.

He turned back to face Scott. Mr. Tanner could be rough, but he was also tender-hearted. He was struggling to say something, so Scott waited patiently.

Finally, he said, "You gave me a great gift today, Scott. I guess I forget sometimes. Thanks for reminding me... well... how we should treat each other."

With that, he stopped and just looked at Scott. Enough had been said. He reached out to shake, but instead took Scott's hand in both of his.

"Merry Christmas."

"Merry Christmas to you, Mr. Tanner."

Mr. Tanner left. Scott stood at the window and watched as him as he exited the building and crossed the street, head held high and smiling.

He turned back to the faded picture and gave it one long, last look, putting his hand carefully on the old frame.

"Thanks, Ben.   And Merry Christmas, from your good friend, Scott," he whispered to himself.

pilogue

Mr. Tanner was right. A great gift was given to him that day. Mr. Tanner did talk to the man with whom he had been so angry. In fact, it did not go very well, but the conversation gave Mr. Tanner yet another gift. He was able to forgive even though the other man was not apologetic. In forgiving, he found peace on the matter and just let the issue go.

What Mr. Tanner did not know at that point was that the man he spoke with would be troubled for some time to come, and eventually would seek Mr. Tanner out and say he was sorry for the thing he had done. Mr. Tanner assured the man that he had forgiven him long ago, and that he was sorry the man had spent so much time in anguish about it, but that he appreciated him coming.

As they shook hands and melted the misunderstanding that had persisted for so long between them, Mr. Tanner asked the man, "If you have a few minutes, may I tell you a story?"

That man was changed as well from that point forward, and so it has continued onward, from one to another to another. Because a young boy listened to his conscience, because a caring father counseled him, because an apology was offered, because hearts were softened, and because forgiveness was given, a great blessing was bestowed upon two young boys that eventually spread out for generations. Today, wherever in the world you can find a relationship which has a thread leading back to the friendship of Scott and Ben, you will find something special, something marked by patience and understanding and forgiveness and love.

Indeed, in that circle of people who have been touched by the story and allowed it to change their feelings and actions toward at least one other soul, there is, as some would say, peace on Earth, and good will toward men.

Acknowledgements

I want to give my thanks to Jane Hughes, who came as a complete blessing to offer her brilliance in editing as well as her artistic talents to create Ben's picture. To Katrina Hughes, who used her keen eye to help us design the cover. To Crickett Willardsen who gave me great help on the cover art.

I also want to pay tribute and offer thanks to those who have not only helped me on this project, but on my entire life's journey. To Mom and Dad, who taught values, and more importantly, lived them in a way that we not only learned them, but loved them. To Bill and Karyn, who edited and suggested with insight and kindness and were tireless in trying to help me work this through. To Bryan, who constantly fed my enthusiasm in this project, and in all things, to reach for life's dreams and who gave me the gift that got me started on the right foot. To Christianne, who never relented in seeing me as a writer and whose complete support in my career change helped me enormously. To Katherine, who has been my #1 cheerleader on this book from the very beginning, pushing me and encouraging me, and who had the vision to suggest the title.

To Loree, who has stood by me, supported me, inspired me, and believed in me in this and in all things, always.

To my extended family and friends who have provided so much enthusiastic backing of me and this effort.

And finally, to God, who has made all things possible and taught me to 'be believing.'

$\mathscr{A}$bout the Author

Bill Bennett grew up in New England. He spent thirty-one years in business, including many years as an executive of various companies and most recently as division president of Franklin Covey. In 2009, Bill decided to spend full time fulfilling his passion of writing, teaching, and consulting. An accomplished leader, speaker and teacher,

Bill has always used stories of everyday, great human character to cut through the detail and reach the hearts of those with whom he's worked.

Bill has spent thirty wonderful years married to Loree Bascom and they have been blessed with four children, ranging from twenty-eight to eleven, as well as two grandchildren.

Bill and his family reside at the base of the Rocky Mountains in Alpine, Utah.

If you wish to contact Bill, he can be reached at:

rwbennett@aol.com

or

5406 West 11000 North
Suite 103-311
Highland, UT 84003-8942

Please feel free to write!